WITHIN THE DARK PLACES

PLACES

Duncan Thompson

First published 2016
by Rowanvale Books Ltd
Imperial House
Trade Street Lane
Cardiff
CF10 5DT
www.rowanvalebooks.com

A CIP catalogue record for this book is available from the British Library.
ISBN: 978-1-910832-27-1

1

The moon was full and bright. The Sea of Tranquility could be clearly seen on this night as summer drew to a close, making way to autumn. Beams of silver light broke through the receding canopy of the forest below.

Towards the edge of the forest a young man began to place fireworks into the dry earth. These were not just any run-of-the-mill, over-the-counter fireworks. These were the type used for large public displays. Several fireworks were placed in a circle. The man was about to place the largest into the centre when the voice of a young woman called him. He turned round to face a small tent centred in a makeshift campsite. From the door of the tent a woman's face peered. She looked to be in her early twenties. Her porcelain skin almost shone in the moonlight, and her long, dark chocolate coloured hair and eyes contrasted strikingly against her pale complexion.

'What are you doing?' she asked, a confused look upon her face.

The man, who was a similar age, with similar facial features, glanced at her with a look of embarrassment and guilt, as if he had been caught doing something naughty. He coughed to clear his throat in order to answer. 'You caught me —' he laughed '— it was meant to be a surprise. I know how much you like fireworks.'

Although this was true, the woman was still a little confused as to what her fellow camper was up to. The expression on her face was clear and prompted further explanation.

The man dropped a silver Zippo cigarette lighter next to the fireworks, with the intention of returning to his plan, and scuttled over to the tent. The woman moved back to allow him inside. The man sat down and pulled a small box from his pocket and lifted the lid. A small diamond ring sat cushioned in the centre. The woman let out a small squeak and quickly covered her mouth with both hands in shock and surprise.

'I was going to light the fireworks and then...' He paused for a moment. 'Well, you know...' He finished the sentence by shrugging his shoulders. The woman squeaked again and then snatched the box. She removed the ring and slipped it onto the ring finger of her left hand. A beaming smile stretched across her face. 'Yes, yes, yes. You know I will.'

She threw her arms round her new fiancé and they kissed passionately, their hands exploring each other's bodies. The kiss was short-lived as the sound of something brushing past the tent killed the romantic atmosphere. The couple sat there for a moment in silence. The sound came again, as something scraped down the waterproof canvas. This time it was accompanied by a shadow darting across the outside of the tent. And then again, but now with a soft whisper.

The woman trembled. 'What was that?'

'I don't know...' The man shrugged. 'It was probably an animal.'

'Go see,' urged the woman, pushing her fiancé out of the tent door.

Once clear of the tent the man stood up and looked round 360 degrees, but the forest was too dense and too dark to be able to see any farther than a few feet.

The woman sat rocking back and forth, her bare legs curled against her chest. She screamed as a dirty hand burst its way into the tent. 'Pass me the torch,' demanded the voice of her fiancé from outside the tent. The woman slapped the man's hand and then passed him the torch which had been tied to the overhead tent pole.

The man shone the torch over the roof of the tent; the beam of light cut through the darkness and into the trees. There was nothing except for tree branches and their shadows. The man was about to climb back inside the tent when the faint sound of laughter could be heard beyond the foliage. 'Go see,' his fiancée urged again.

The groom-to-be hesitantly walked deeper into the woods, but the noise was no closer than it had been before. He turned his head back towards the campsite every few steps, eager to return to his lover and finish what they had started. He watched the tent grow smaller and smaller as he progressed deeper into the woods, until it disappeared out of view, consumed by the dark.

After several more yards the man stood still; the only sound he could hear was his own anxious breath and his heart drumming against his chest. Infuriated at wasting his time he shook his head and turned, making his way back towards the campsite.

The clearing came back into view, but the tent was now dismantled. The groundsheet and canvas were torn to shreds, tent poles were bent and strewn across the ground, rucksacks and clothing scattered, the campfire extinguished, and the bride-to-be nowhere to be seen. The man froze with disbelief, his pulse quickening with panic. He called out for his fiancée, but there was no response. He called again, and then a third time, as loud as he could, straining his voice, but there was still no response. The man looked round frantically, the torchlight darting left to right.

A number of worst-case scenarios crossed his mind. He knew the girl too well to know this wasn't a prank. Not on her part, anyway. But the most terrifying thought was to question what her father would do to him if he returned from the woods alone without any explanation as to where his daughter had gone.

The man was about to call again, his throat sore and dry, his voice shaking with fear. A shadow dashed past the corner of his eye. He spun to the right, but saw nothing. Then, a shadow dashed across the corner of the left eye. Only this time, the man was able to make out the distinct silhouette of a person. Feebly, he called for his fiancée, asking if it was her, although his heart told him it wasn't. The sound of laughter came in reply.

From behind, something pushed into the man with force, causing him to drop his torch. The impact of it hitting the ground caused the battery to shake loose. The light flickered and died.

Now, surrounded by darkness, the man could see no more than arm's length in front of him. However, he could still hear the sound of footsteps running circles around him, feeling an arctic draught blow across his face as they did so. Then he felt something else, something striking his face, something which made him cry out in pain. Reacting, he reached for his cheek; sticky blood ran between his fingertips, but the wound was oddly ice-cold. The same pain came again, this time across his left shoulder blade. He then felt a sharp blow as something clawed at his chest, tearing his shirt and the flesh beneath. Again the wound was frostbitten, almost numb.

He stood still for a moment. Although frozen by fear he could sense something at his feet. An icy grip constricted round his ankles and then, with force, his feet were pulled out from under him. He lay flat on his back — whatever was in the shadows still had a hold of his legs. It took a moment for the man to realise, but he was now being dragged across the ground. The speed at which he was being pulled increased. Fallen branches and stones were scratching and grazing his body. He continued to be pulled farther into the woods, through the trees, deeper into the darkness and into oblivion.

A cloud floated across the moon and all was still.

2

Joe stood hunched over, his palms resting on his thighs, trying to catch his breath, each lungful of air causing his chest to tighten. His heart pounded against his breastbone like a pneumatic drill. Every muscle in his body was burning, but for now the adrenaline kept the pain at bay. But it wasn't the pain that was the problem — it was the fatigue.

Right now, all he wanted to do was lie down in the thick, cold, oozy mud he was standing in, close his eyes and go to sleep. But he couldn't. He wouldn't. There were people who were depending on him and one person in particular he could never let down.

Behind him, Joe could hear heavy footsteps, the footsteps of many rather than a single person. Some of the footsteps sounded to be closing in at a rapidly increasing pace; others seemed to trip and stumble. And within only a few short seconds, Joe could now hear the erratic breathing of the pursuers.

After tearing through burning bales of hay, wading through ice-cold water and climbing a multitude of electrified fences, to name a few of the challenges he had already faced today, Joe now looked up at the final obstacle which blocked his path. It was a ten-foot-tall vertical wooden wall. All Joe had to do was scale the wall, drop down the other side and make a 100 metre sprint to freedom.

Joe lifted his shirt and wiped the cocktail of sweat and mud from his brow; the salty brown liquid soaked into the paper badge which displayed his runner's number. Looking over his shoulder, Joe could see the other runners closing in on his lead. He took a deep breath and prepared to climb the wall.

Although the wall was only ten feet tall, when Joe stared at the top it appeared to be more like fifty. He took a few steps backward, gritted his teeth and darted head-on towards the wall, taking a jump up at it. As his feet connected with the flat surface he pushed back, his long muscular legs propelling him higher. Joe reached up, his height helping him to grip tightly to the top of the wall. He pulled himself up, the muscles of his lean frame tightening. The pain he had managed to hold off for so long now burned through his arms and shoulders with a vengeance, causing him to snarl as he lifted himself onto the top of the wall.

On the other side of the wall, three feet down from the top, was a small ledge. Joe sat for a moment to catch his breath, he could hear the few remaining runners taking their turn at the wall; a dull thump-thump against the wooden slats. Joe stood up and, turning his head, could see several of them already scrambling over the top. He couldn't stop now or he would lose his lead. He was about to jump down when he heard one of the runners on the other side of the wall scream out loud. Joe looked back over the edge to see a small slender man struggling to reach the top. Joe reached over and offered his hand. The small runner reached up and clutched Joe's wrist. Joe pulled with all his remaining strength, his biceps bulging and his heels digging into the ledge to stop him from being pulled over. The small runner clambered over the top and flopped onto the ledge.

WITHIN THE DARK PLACES

The last of the remaining runners now scaled the wall, leaving Joe and the small runner the only two remaining competitors to complete the final obstacle. Joe shook his head for a second as an air of despair washed over him. Then he caught sight of the finish line and its distance from the other runners, who were now beginning to lose their pace. There was a small chance he could take back his lead. Together Joe and the small runner jumped down from the ledge, but the smaller runner didn't have the strength to keep his balance; his foot slid from under him, twisting his ankle. Joe helped the man to his feet and, placing his arm across his own shoulder, he helped the runner to the finish line. All hope of regaining his lead was lost.

***

Supporting his injured opponent, Joe staggered across the finish line. The man broke free of his support and shook his hand. 'Thank you,' he gasped, catching his breath.

Joe released his grip and placed his hands on his hips as he caught his own breath. 'Yeah, anytime,' he mumbled. He was angry with himself for giving up his lead and even more so for finishing last, but he knew he would have felt a hell of a lot worse if he had just left the guy to lie there in the mud, not when the injured man had come so far. It was an achievement in itself to even reach the finish line, let alone be the first to cross it.

The small runner limped away towards the spectators to find his family. Joe shook his head and cursed himself again for giving away his lead. He took a deep breath and licked his lips, 'I couldn't leave a man behind,' he muttered, justifying his actions to himself.

'Joseph!' an excited voice cried from within the

crowd. With the exception of his mother, only one other person called him Joseph. It was his fiancée, Linda.

Joe, as he would always introduce himself, and as he was called by everyone else, staggered over to where Linda was standing. Next to her was his younger brother, Tony.

Although brothers, Joe and Tony were polar opposites; Tony was much shorter and his arms and chest were thin, lacking definition. A flabby belly had also made an appearance over the last few years. However, the pair could still be recognised as brothers; they shared the same facial features — a heritage passed down from their estranged Italian father.

Joe's personality was outgoing and he loved being outdoors, taking part in extreme sports from an early age. He wanted to join the Royal Marines when he left school, but stayed at home for Tony.

When their father left, the elder brother was drafted into helping his mother raise Tony by stepping into the absent Joseph Senior's shoes. It was not long after their parents separated that Tony was diagnosed with epilepsy and, shortly after that, was told he had asthma. Even as an adult he was still dependent on his inhaler and medication. In those early days though, he was much more prone to severe seizures. For that reason, the boys' mother wrapped her younger son in a cotton blanket, shielding him from the world. As a result, he was shy and had a nervous disposition.

It was because of Tony that Joe entered the Iron Man competition on an annual basis; it was a ten kilometre run, with obstacles that pushed you to your limits, and he had been certain this time, more determined than ever, that he would finish first. But as much as Joe would have loved the glory of being the first to cross the finish line, he had raised enough money for epilepsy awareness by being one of the few entrants to actually complete the course. And after all, that was the reason he had entered to begin with.

3

The hatch-back slowly rolled to a halt. The tyres were grey from dust the car had collected as it travelled down the dirt track, but now the road came to an end.

Inside, the car was cramped. Joe was sat behind the wheel, switching off the engine. Tony was in the passenger seat. He had been quiet all morning, barely uttering a word. Joe sensed there was something going on in his brother's mind, but when he approached the subject Tony would either deny his mood or claim he was simply feeling tired.

On the back seat of the car sat Charlie. While Charlie shared Joe's enthusiasm for fitness, he didn't care for the outdoors and his gym regime centred on looking good rather than improving one's health and wellbeing. He certainly carried more muscle than Joe, but he was several inches shorter and considerably more narcissistic. From his bottom lip sprouted a blond soul patch, which he stroked habitually, grinning to himself each time he did.

If a vote was taken on the least popular member of the group, Charlie would be elected. He had once made a sexist comment in front of Linda and in return she'd called him a rude, obnoxious, selfish ape. In truth it was a fair description. However, he had been friends with Joe since starting school and a strong loyalty had grown between the pair.

Next to Charlie sat Mike. He was more on par with Tony; he had a slim, wiry build and wore glasses, thick in lens and frame. What he lacked in fitness he made up for with enthusiasm. While they had all been friends for many years, Mike was still the newest member of the group and at times he still felt the need to prove himself worthy of their friendship. He would allow himself to be the group's errand-boy. If you needed something, any favour, Mike was your man.

'End of the line,' said Joe, as he pulled the key from the ignition. 'We walk from here.'

Charlie moaned, 'This is your last free weekend before you get hitched — why you would want to spend it trekking round the woods, I'll never know. We should be in Amsterdam, sampling the local delicacies.'

Mike agreed. 'Charlie has a point. The more traditional stag weekend would be somewhere…' He paused, trying to find the right word. 'Lively.'

Joe shook his head. 'Guys, I'm through with all that sort of thing now. I just want to spend a quiet weekend with my best friends. No fuss, nothing exciting. Just keep it simple.'

'We should still be going to Amsterdam,' Charlie muttered to himself as he massaged his right bicep, checking for any further growth since his last workout — heaven forbid it had shrunk overnight.

At the end of the dirt track was an iron gate which opened up into a meadow. Across the meadow was Druid Wood.

***

The town of Raven's Peak, where Joe and Tony had spent most of their lives, sat on the east slope of a valley. The valley itself formed part of a larger network of moorland. At the foot of the valley was Druid Wood, which stretched the entire length of the valley, while also climbing up either side.

At the heart of the forest was a circle of stone tablets, bearing a strong resemblance to Stonehenge. The folklore told of how Druids had used this area as a place of worship for their practices. Later, local historians had discovered a network of man-made tunnels running under the woods which had led to one of Raven's Peak's manor houses. Over time, the stones, the tunnels and their history had been forgotten. The stone tablets were left to be eroded by the elements, gather moss and become hidden amongst the leaves. The entrance to the tunnel from the manor house had been sealed off to stop anyone entering. Now the only manmade structure that received human attention were the numerous electric pylons which stretched through the valley.

The woods were also home to deer, as well as a variety of other woodland creatures. However, this lured numerous poachers to the spot in past years. While the police had cracked down on the poaching, the numerous bear traps, snares and trip wires had all remained hidden, still armed and still dangerous.

Raven's Peak council had decided it wasn't worth the time or the expense to find and disarm the traps. Instead, the solution was to fence off that particular area of the woods. If someone fell afoul of one of the traps, the council avoided any responsibility as it had placed sufficient warning signs urging people to keep out.

***

The party unloaded their camping equipment from the boot of the car and, jumping the gate, proceeded to march across the meadow.

When they were halfway across the meadow Joe took his mobile phone from his pocket and stared at the display as he prepared to dial. The message 'No Network' sat ominously in the top right hand corner of the screen. Joe swore under his breath.

'Tony, have you got any reception?'

Tony checked his own phone and shook his head, 'No, sorry.'

Joe turned to Mike. 'What about you?'

'That's a negative, Captain.' He pointed a finger to the power lines that stretched overhead. 'These cables cause too much interference. There is no chance of getting a signal while they run above our heads.'

Charlie looked puzzled. 'Why do you need to know if anyone has any reception?'

Joe turned to face him. 'Just want to check in with Linda. Let her know we arrived safely.' Joe hadn't noticed but the mention of Linda's name caused Tony to flinch.

Charlie scoffed in disbelief at what he was hearing as they continued to trek through the meadow.

The sun was beginning to set as they reached the wood. A wooden fence circled the perimeter, but a stile granted them access. One by one they stepped up onto the stile, taking a stride over the top of the fence, and dropped down the other side into the trees.

As the sun began to set, the shadow of the tree branches began to stretch across the meadow. A light breeze caused the trees to sway gently. The motion caused the shadows to resemble a bony, clawed hand, which appeared to eerily beckon would-be travellers into the darkness of Druid Wood.

4

After a short hike through the woods the party came to a clearing. There were signs that this area had been used as a campsite recently: a bent tent pole or two, a tattered rucksack and a broken torch. Embers in what had once been a fire-pit still smouldered.

'This will do,' said Joe and he dropped his backpack.

'Thank God!' Tony sighed as he sat on a fallen tree trunk.

'It looks like someone recently set up camp here,' Mike observed, 'maybe only a day or two ago?' He cast his eyes over the remnants of the former camp. 'Left in a hurry,' he muttered under his breath.

'Right, let's get the beers out!' said Charlie, excitedly rubbing his hands together. Several six-packs emerged from his backpack, with very little else remaining.

'Where is your camping equipment?' asked Tony. 'Didn't you bring a tent?'

'Nope,' was the blunt response from Charlie. 'Thought I'd bunk in with you.'

Tony wasn't pleased at the thought; in fact, the idea repulsed him. He had shared a tent with Charlie once before and it hadn't been a pleasant experience. But, being Tony, he was too timid to say anything opposing.

Joe made another attempt to call home. Holding the handset to his ear while waiting for the call to connect, he wandered round the campsite, kicking up stones and earth. His foot connected with something that was not rock or dirt. The best Joe could make of it, as it was flung into the undergrowth, was that it was cylindrical in shape. He looked down to see a handful of fireworks scattered on the ground. An object, hidden under the leaves amongst the fireworks, reflected what little daylight remained into Joe's eyes. He crouched down and brushed away the leaves to reveal an expensive looking Zippo cigarette lighter. Curiosity ordered him to pick it up for a closer inspection. The telephone call now connected and Joe pushed the lighter into his trouser pocket without a second thought.

'Linda?'

A voice responded, but the screeching static disguised whatever had been said.

'Linda,' Joe tried again, 'just calling to tell you we have arrived.' No response, only more static and interference. As before, Tony glanced over with a look of panic. The phone beeped twice as the call disconnected, then silence. Joe angrily stared at his phone. 'The UK's biggest network my arse!' he snarled as he slipped the phone back into his pocket and returned to his friends to help set up camp.

Upon realising the call had failed, Tony relaxed a little; whatever was on his mind apparently concerned Linda.

5

The sun had now set, making way for a clear night sky. The moon was bright and full, and lunar light trickled through the canopy of Druid Wood. The cry of owls and various other creatures that inhabited the woods now filled the air. The woods were more alive now than they had been at any time throughout the day.

Mike had managed to get a fire started and the stag party sat round it, exchanging stories and jokes while guzzling beers. Joe played with the cigarette lighter he had found earlier; igniting the flame, closing the lid, and then igniting the flame again. He repeated the cycle over several times. Tony had learned that his older brother showed this kind of repetitive behaviour when he was angry or frustrated, but dared not show it — and right now he was both. This made Tony even more paranoid that his brother knew the secret he harboured. Joe had tried several times since finding the lighter to call home, but the calls would not connect. He tried using his friends' mobile phones, but the outcome was still the same.

Charlie was beginning to grow annoyed that Joe was paying more attention to the lighter than his friends. 'Just throw that thing away, will you?' he snapped, and then took another gulp of his beer.

Joe looked up, slightly startled, as if he had been pulled from a trance. He muttered something that resembled the word sorry, and proceeded to place the lighter back in his pocket.

'I don't know why you want that thing anyway,' Charlie said, 'you don't smoke.'

Joe sighed. 'I know. Sorry. It was just a distraction really.'

'From what?' Charlie asked the question, but knew the answer.

Joe had promised Linda that he would phone home. Charlie had learnt over many years of their friendship that when Joe promised something he would not rest easy until the promise had been fulfilled.

'You're right. We came here to have a good time,' Joe said reluctantly. He looked across to Mike who was sat next to a pack of beer.

Mike placed the can he was sipping from on the ground. 'Yes, boss.'

'Can you pass me a beer, please?' asked Joe. Mike reached down for a can and shuffled the position of his feet as he passed it towards Joe. As he did this the tip of his shoe caught the can he had been drinking from. It toppled over and a river of lager flowed from the rim, hissing and fizzing as it meandered through the leaves and dirt towards the fire.

The fire hissed and the flames died from the baptism of Special Brew. What remained of the embers were now too wet to set alight again. The fire would need to be rebuilt.

'Well done!' The sarcasm, naturally, came from Charlie.

Joe chuckled. 'I wouldn't worry about it, Mike. We've got plenty of torches.'

Tony looked at the sodden charcoal. 'It's a shame really. I liked the open fire.'

Mike stood up. 'I'll get more wood, some sticks

and branches and things. I'll build another one in no time,' he proposed with enthusiasm.

'Really, it's fine.' Joe made a gesture with his hand, suggesting that Mike should sit back down.

'No. Really, I insist.' Mike staggered towards his tent, then rummaged round inside for his torch. He emerged, torch in hand and a smile on his face. 'I won't be long,' he said as he skipped into the trees. The light from the torch danced for a few seconds then faded as Mike disappeared into the night.

***

A girl with long brown hair, dressed in nothing but a t-shirt and underwear, began to stir from a deep sleep, relieved to have woken from a nightmare. Her eyes adjusted to the dark, and she realised her surroundings were the same as they had been for the last two days.

The damp cool air of the cave filled her lungs. Her arms ached; hot flushes of pain raced through the muscles from them being stretched above her head. Something bound her to the roof of the cave.

In her mind, recent events were a muddle. The last thing she clearly remembered was being sat in a tent, talking to her boyfriend. Then another memory came to her; he was no longer her boyfriend, he was now her fiancé. Yes, that was right, she remembered he had proposed and she had accepted. Then, in between the marriage proposal and waking up in the dark with her hands bound above her head, there was mostly blank space. However, she seemed to recall her fiancé was in the cave with her at first. Then something... She couldn't remember. All she knew now was her husband-to-be was no longer there.

The girl had always been strong-willed, with a positive, can-do, optimistic attitude. At first she had tried to escape and was confident she could, but no matter how hard she'd tried she could not free herself from her restraints; her slight frame was not strong enough. And then there was the shadow that lurked in the darkness with her.

Although the cave was pitch-black, she could just about make out the silhouette of someone — or something — circling her. And then there was the smell. It was something she had smelt before, but couldn't quite place it; there was a recollection of high school chemistry lessons.

Whatever was lurking in the dark, it had been here with her the whole time, even when her fiancé had still been there. Occasionally she would feel its smooth hand touch her cheek, caressing her soft skin, slowly moving down to her breasts.

The hand was ice-cold to the touch. Not only on her skin, but it would also send a chill down to her bones, surging through her body. Whenever the hand moved over her chest, towards her heart, she would pass out, but not before she could feel its fingers penetrate her skin.

The worst part was the nightmares that occurred when she drifted out of consciousness. She could not recall images, only feelings. Feelings of anger and hate, feelings of loneliness and hopelessness. Emotions she had rarely experienced before, but was now overcome with them. It was the nightmares that were slowly killing her high-spirited nature, replacing it with a dark despair.

6

At first Mike struggled to find decent firewood. Many of the sticks and fallen branches had begun to rot under the leaf-litter. After some searching, however, he managed to find good quality dry wood.

With as much firewood as he could carry under his left arm, and the torch held in his right hand, he decided to head back to the camp. In his enthusiasm he had not realised how deep into the woods he had wandered. He shone the torch to his left and then to his right, trying to get his bearings, and then turned around, hoping he was returning in the direction he had come from.

Behind him came a faint whisper, the sound of his name being carried on the breeze. Mike spun round and shone the torch into the trees ahead, squinting through the lenses of his glasses, trying to see beyond the beam of light. There was nothing there.

Concluding that the voice he'd heard was only the wind, Mike continued on his way. The moment he put that thought to bed the whispering started up again. This time there was more than one voice and he had no doubt that someone was calling him.

Mike placed the wood on the ground and shone the torch in all directions. Something moved up ahead. Mike directed the torch to a briar-bush where his eyes caught the movement. A white bird shot up from the brambles, wailing like a spirit rising from a grave as it soared up into the treetops out of harm's way. Mike gasped as his whole body jumped and his heart raced. Then, doubled over, head between his knees trying to catch his breath, he began to laugh. He stood up straight and took a deep breath. The whispers returned.

***

Beer was now running low. Empty tins and discarded crisp packets now littered the campsite. Charlie was midway through one of his racist, sexist jokes.

Tony winced, but not at the bad taste of the joke. His head began to throb and instinctively he pinched the bridge of his nose in an attempt to relieve the pain. Joe, noticing his younger brother's behaviour, cast a watchful eye. Charlie continued to tell his joke and the moment he delivered the punch line Tony's shoulders jerked upward. The convulsion could have been mistaken for a hiccup, but Joe knew it wasn't.

'Tony?' Joe asked with concern in his voice.

Tony's shoulders jerked again. He was having a myoclonic seizure. 'I'm okay, just give me a minute,' he answered, waving his hand in front of Joe's face. His shoulders jerked again.

Joe knew this type of seizure should be nothing to worry about. It was quite common for people diagnosed with epilepsy to experience this. The seizure would pass after a few moments, without any need for any medical intervention, but there had been times when they were growing up that this had led to the uncontrollable movements of tonic-clonic seizure.

A worried look shot across Charlie's face. 'Christ,

he's not going to have a fit, is he?'

Tony shook his head. 'No, I'm okay now. I'll be alright.'

The shoulder jerks now stopped and Tony smiled, but the jovial atmosphere had subsided. In that moment, Joe realised that it had been a considerable length of time since Mike had left to collect firewood, and he had yet to return.

***

The whispers were coming from all directions now. Mike shone the torch frantically, trying to establish the source of the voices. He didn't recognise them, but they clearly knew him. They weren't just calling him by his first name now; they were chanting his full name, including the middle ones. Apart from his immediate family only Joe and Tony knew...

'Joe! Is that you?' Mike called out, but the only response was another whisper. 'Tony?' It had to be them, some kind of a practical joke. But practical jokes weren't the brothers' forte. It was, however, the sort of thing you could expect from Charlie.

Charlie!

'Charlie, you swine! Give it up now. I know it's you.'

The torch light flickered erratically as the battery began to die.

Mike cursed under his breath, slapping the butt of the torch, as if somehow this would miraculously give the battery a boost of energy. It didn't. The light blinked one last time and then it was gone. The glow of the bulb's element slowly faded. Mike mumbled several curse words, which, if his mother had heard him, would have still caused her to wash his mouth out, even at the age of twenty-six — and not just metaphorically.

Even though the torch was now dead, the light

from the moon was strong enough to allow Mike to see a few yards ahead of him. He was about to pick up his collection of sticks and branches and make his way hastily back to the camp, when he saw the shadow of something moving up ahead.

Mike paused, squinting through the thick lenses of his glasses. Whatever it was, it looked human in shape. Mike stood still — so did the shadow. The shadow was elongated, its legs and arms long and out of proportion to the head and body — like a stick-man. Due to the distraction of the shadow, Mike hadn't noticed that the whispering had now stopped. Even the woods themselves had also fallen silent; gone were the bird songs and animal calls.

Mike continued to squint, tilting his head. The head of the shadow mirrored the movement. Mike took a step back. The shadow took a step back, its legs and arms stretched out farther. Mike now had a hunch as to what this thing was and began to relax a little. To test his theory he raised his arms above his head. The shadow raised its arms above its head. Mike performed a little knees-up jig. The shadow performed the same dance.

'Jumping at my own shadow,' Mike muttered, chuckling to himself. But there was something more important than the silence he had also failed to notice. The moon wasn't behind him to cast a shadow out in front, it was to his right. He bent down to finally pick up the firewood and then he saw his own shadow cast to the left.

Mike jolted upright with fright. Surely it must have been his own shadow he had been playing with? Wasn't it? The shadow was still where it had been, beyond the trees, but now it stood completely still, no longer mimicking his movements. Mike trembled; a cold sweat ran across his brow. He walked backward, slowly. The shadow walked forward at the same speed.

Still walking backward, Mike began to pick up speed. The shadow continued to move forward, also picking up speed. He looked round frantically, hoping his friends would now reveal themselves, like the hosts of a hidden camera show. They made no such appearance.

Now Mike's instinct was to run. He was turning his body when he saw the shadow had gone. Mike scanned the trees, holding his breath, but there was no sign of it. He exhaled and in the blink of an eye the shadow stood directly in front of him, cold air radiating from it. Goosepimples crawled all over Mike's skin. He could feel the hair on the back of his arms and neck stand to attention.

Mike now knew this thing was not a mere shadow. It was certainly shadowlike, appearing two dimensional in shape, as if cut from a single piece of jet black cloth.

The entity wore no facial features, only a blank, black, head-shaped canvas. Even though it had no eyes, Mike could sense it was staring directly into his own. It was a similar height to Mike, but its limbs were still stretched out of proportion. Its long, thin legs did not appear to have feet; they only ended at a point which seemed to stick into the ground. As much as its arms were out of proportion to the body, the hands and fingers were even more distorted. The fingers themselves came to a point, clawlike.

The creature bent forward, lowering its head; its arms reached outward and upward like an eagle expanding its wings. Although it had no mouth or nose, Mike could hear it breathing, a wheezy, gravelly sound. Its breath filled Mike's nose with the smell of rotten eggs. It was the smell of sulphur. And then it screamed.

The high-pitched shrill echoed throughout the trees. A seismic shockwave travelled through Mike's entire body, the scream piercing his ears. He stood now, frozen with terror — catatonic.

The creature's head bobbed up and down, rubbing against Mike's chest. There was something very animal about this, like a dog sniffing a stranger to ascertain if they were friend or foe. As it touched Mike, ice-cold pains shot through his body.

It took a few steps back then screamed once more. Mike was still frozen with fear. The shadow-creature raised an arm and struck Mike, flinging him into the undergrowth, its claws cutting him along his jaw and neck.

Mike hit the ground with a thud, shaking him from his state of catatonia. He scrambled to his knees then reached to feel the wounds on his face and neck. The cuts were cold to the touch and intricate crystals formed under his fingertips, the wounds resembling frostbite. Then Mike realised he couldn't see. Not that he was blind, but the world was an out of focus blur. His glasses had been knocked from his head. He scrambled round on his hands and knees, frantically searching for them. The fear of what his mother would do to him if he lost them would not escape his mind.

The creature continued to howl, but this time the screams did not appear to be directed at Mike. It appeared to be calling out in a way in which a wolf would call to the rest of its pack for support.

For as much as Mike was short-sighted, he was still able to see more creatures manifest from the shadows of the trees, bushes and rocks that formed the Druid Wood. This thing was not alone.

As Mike scrambled on all fours in search of his spectacles, eager not to displease Mummy, a black cloud began to blanket him.

7

Joe passed a torch to Tony and another to Charlie. He glanced at his watch, trying to establish how long Mike had been gone, but he couldn't remember what time it had been when Mike had actually left them. Charlie was about to protest at the idea of going into the dark woods to search for their friend. He figured Mike would return soon enough. That, and the fact he was drunk; certainly in no condition to slog through the wild on a search and rescue mission.

A terrifying, high-pitched, ear-penetrating scream filled the air. The three men instantly turned in a northerly direction to where the noise appeared to come from.

'What the hell was that?' Charlie had sobered up instantly.

'I have no idea,' gasped Joe as he switched on his torch; a high-powered industrial lamp he used for work. The beam of light illuminated the ground by his feet. 'We've got to find Mike.' He paused for a moment. 'That sound could have been Mike. He could be hurt.'

Charlie shook his head. 'That didn't sound like Mike.'

Joe placed a hand on Tony's shoulder. 'You okay? You can stay here if you're not feeling up to this.'

'Yeah, I'm fine. Let's go.' It was a lie. He wasn't okay — he was terrified. Terrified of the woods and terrified of the darkness. Terrified that something bad had happened to Mike. Terrified of the scream they had just heard and he knew he would be terrified of whatever had made it. But in spite of these fears and the awkwardness he had been feeling in Joe's presence over the past day, he knew his big brother would still look after him when trouble raised its ugly head. A second scream filled the air.

Torches in hand, they made their way farther into the woods in the direction of the screams. After roughly quarter of a mile they stopped to reassess the situation.

Charlie shook his head. 'He can't have gone this far, surely?'

Joe shrugged. 'I don't know, possibly?' He then called out for Mike.

Tony, wanting to be useful, did the same. 'Mike!' he yelled. 'You there?'

Charlie rolled his eyes, but with no other ideas to suggest, he joined the chorus. 'Mike, you four-eyed —'

Joe smacked him across the back of his head. 'That's enough!'

Charlie grimaced and mocked a punch to the back of Joe's head as he walked past.

They continued to walk north several more yards when something cracked under Charlie's foot. He looked down, shining the torch at his feet. He moved his foot back to reveal a pair of broken glasses — the left lens missing, the right leg twisted under the frame. He knelt down to pick the glasses up and shone the torch on to them. Even in their state of disrepair, they were undoubtedly Mike's.

'Erm, guys...' Charlie was unable to find the words to complete the sentence.

Joe and Tony turned and their eyes fell on the

glasses that Charlie held in front of his face. Joe snatched them from Charlie. 'Damn it. Mike, where are you?' he muttered.

At that moment something in the treeline caught Tony's eye. A shape shimmered against the tree trunks. He pointed the torch in the direction of the silhouette, but as the light travelled across the ground the shape disappeared. Tony shrugged and lowered the torch. The shape appeared once more, but as quickly as Tony lifted the torch for another look it disappeared once again. He lowered the torch, only more slowly and this time he didn't take his eyes away from the spot where he had seen the silhouette. Once the light was at his feet, the shape reappeared. And it wasn't alone.

Two more shapes emerged from the trees. All three appeared human in shape, or at least more or less, thought Tony, but their limbs were exaggerated. Tony was about to conclude the silhouettes were his, Joe's and Charlie's shadows, but then two more silhouettes materialised.

Tony yanked his brother's arm. Joe turned, passing the broken glasses back to Charlie (who threw them back on the ground). 'Yeah? What...' The sight of the five shadows caused him to pause. He shone the torch in their direction, but as they had done with Tony, they quickly disappeared just before the light hit the trees where they stood. 'Who's there?' Joe shouted.

A whisper on the breeze called his name.

Charlie now shone his torch in the same direction. A rustling in the wind called Charlie's name. 'Who wants to know?' Charlie shouted with bravado.

Tony reached out across both Joe and Charlie, pushing their arms down to lower the torches. 'Look,' he whispered and pointed to the trees, as the beams of light travelled back towards the group. Two of the shadows reappeared simultaneously, then the third, followed by the final two reappearing together.

'Hey!' Charlie shouted, throwing his torch to the ground as he marched towards the shadows. The shadows marched towards him. Joe leaped forward to take hold of his friend, pulling him back by his shoulder.

Charlie cast Joe an angry stare. Joe glared back, trumping Charlie's stare with a self-elected seniority. They both now stood still. The shadows stood still.

'We don't want any bother,' Joe declared, 'we're just looking for our friend. Have you seen him? He's twenty-six, slimly built, sandy-blond hair... He was wearing a pair of glasses.'

'Michael...' It was the whisper on the wind again. Tony could sense the whisper belonged to the shadows, but they weren't its source. It seemed to emit from the highest branches of the trees, from the rocks which protruded out from the dirt. It was all around them, like the night itself.

'Yes,' Joe called. 'Michael. Mike. You have seen him?'

The central shadow screeched. It was the cry they had heard before. As the howl echoed, two more of the shadows screeched and then the final two, to create a round of chorus. The three friends instantly covered their ears, wincing, their eyes tightly shut. A tear ran down Tony's cheek.

With the cries continuing, Joe dared to open his eyes to see the shadows descending upon them. 'Run!' he screamed. He sprinted back in the direction they had come from, pulling Tony by the arm. Charlie, treading on Mike's glasses again, pushing them into the mud, glanced over his shoulder as he followed Joe and Tony. He saw several more shadows appear. He counted at least eight, nine, maybe even ten of them giving chase.

8

After a frantic sprint through the trees, ducking under low-hanging branches, dodging tree trunks and hurdling over rocks, they stumbled back into the campsite. They appeared to have lost whatever it was they had encountered.

Joe and Charlie caught their breath quickly enough, but the adrenaline still pumped furiously through their veins. Tony wasn't in good shape, however. He was soaked from head to toe in sweat, his thighs and calves cramped, and he wheezed terribly as he tried to catch his breath. He desperately fumbled in his pockets for his inhaler. Once located, he quickly brought it to his lips and took two puffs. Joe cast a concerned eye upon him. 'Are you going to be okay?'

'Yes.' Tony nodded. 'I'll be okay now.' His breathing was slowly returning to normal. 'What on earth was that?' He still asked the question even though he knew no one could offer a real answer.

Joe shook his head. 'I have no idea, but we need to find Mike — and quick.'

'We can't go back in there!' Tony protes need to go get help. Get the police or someo'

'We can't do that, not without trekking b car to be able to make the phone call. Even have to sit and wait for them to show up. We need to find Mike now.'

Tony wasn't convinced. 'But we have no idea what those things were. They could have Mike.' He began to blubber. 'They could have killed him. They could kill us!' The last sentence left his mouth in hysterics.

'I'll tell you what they were,' interrupted Charlie. 'They were a couple of clowns in Morphsuits. For all we know, Mike is in on it. It's the sort of joke he would try and pull.'

'But what was that noise? How were they making that screeching sound?' Tony was convinced there was something supernatural lurking in the woods.

Charlie made a suggestion. 'They've got a couple of air-horns or something.'

Charlie and Tony both looked at Joe, expecting him to make a final decision as to what their next move would be. Do they stay or do they go?

Joe glanced at his watch, and then fiddled in his pocket, playing with the lighter he found earlier. Keeping his hands busy helped him to focus.

'Okay,' he said, almost to himself. 'We look for Mike. We'll split, so we can cover more ground. Meet back here in two hours. If we haven't found him then we go get help.' He could tell Tony was scared. Joe had seen that look on his face many times when they were growing up. 'Listen, why don't you stay here, in case he comes back?' Joe said, trying to assure his little brother that everything would be okay. 'We'll be back in two hours, no later. If Mike does turn up, try and call me. I know this place is a dead-zone for signal, but at least try.'

Tony didn't speak, he simply nodded and tightened his grip on his torch.

'Charlie?' Joe glanced over to Charlie who, pumped with adrenaline, was now more than eager to commence the search for their missing comrade.

'Yes, boss?' he replied.

'Why don't you head west, making your way up the old poachers' trail?'

Charlie nodded. 'What about you?'

Joe licked his lips; they were becoming dry and chapped. 'I'm going to head east, towards the old druid temple.' He took a deep breath, exaggerating the exhale. He looked back at Tony. 'Two hours,' he said softly.

***

Mike staggered through the woods, his memory scrambled. Images came to him in flashes here and there: being dragged through the woods, a sense of being in a cave or perhaps underground, darkness, his tyrannical mother (although these flashbacks seemed more dreamlike; the worst memories of his mother magnified) and then more darkness. And now there only seemed to be darkness — inside and out.

He wandered on aimlessly without any real idea of where he was going or why. The only clarity he had was the haunting melody that now sang in his head; voices he now followed and obeyed.

9

It took Charlie about fifteen minutes to find his way to the poachers' trail, the pathway meandering back and forth as it stretched up the steep face of the valley. A barbed-wire fence ran the length of the valley and through the woods. Where the fence crossed the trail a battered wooden sign hung from the rusted wire. Although the wood was rotten, green with moss and the red paint now faded, flakes of it peeling away, it still clearly read: DANGER —KEEP OUT!

The fence was about six feet high; the barbed wire that stretched the distance of the fence sat at the top, a few inches above Charlie's head. He contemplated climbing it, but the thought of tearing the palms of his hands on rusted barbed-wire convinced him otherwise. He then realised that the fence, in its current state, would not hold his weight, especially when he reached the top. The idea of being wrapped in the barbed-wire was even less appealing.

He stood and pondered the situation for a moment; maybe he should just turn round and go back to the campsite?

On the other side of the fence, farther along the trail, something darted between the trees. Charlie shone the torch in the direction of the something, but whatever it was, it was gone. Then there came the sound of laughter. It was a childlike giggle, which appeared to mock Charlie.

'You can't catch me. Neener-neener-neener.'

'You little...!' Charlie flicked the torchlight across the width of the path, looking for a way round.

The giggling came again. 'You can't catch me. Charlie's too fat! He couldn't catch a cold!'

'I'm going to kick your arses when I get hold of you!'

Charlie continued to scan the fence for a way through to the other side. 'Pigging kids in pigging Morphsuits,' he mumbled to himself. Charlie then noticed that the gap between each row of wire was quite deep. Perhaps, if he could pry it apart a little, he might fit through.

The wires bent easily enough and Charlie poked his head through, then his torso. He lifted his left leg over, holding onto the fence for balance, and then his right leg followed. He found he couldn't drop his right foot to the ground; it hung suspended in the air. He twisted his body round and shone the torch over the lower part of the right leg and his right foot. The bottom of his trouser leg was caught on a bit of wire. He jerked his leg away from the fence, causing the snag to tear up to the knee. The jolt caused Charlie to lose his balance and he fell, face down in the dirt, the palms of his hands hitting the ground with a thud. Fits of laughter rose up from the undergrowth of the woods.

Charlie picked himself up, brushing off the dirt with his hands. He looked down at his right leg to assess the damage to his trousers. 'Damn it!' he grumbled.

He placed the torch in his mouth so to free both hands. He tore off the tattered material that had once been his right trouser leg. He stood for a moment in a pair of half shorts, half trousers, feeling sorry for himself.

The giggling started up again. Charlie bellowed, like a bull that had just seen a red flag, and then he charged along the path.

***

Tony sat shivering on the trunk of the fallen tree he had sat on when they first stopped to set up camp. Although he didn't share a great deal of his big brother's attributes, he could still be quite resourceful.

Tony didn't know what had chased them through the woods earlier, but he remembered that whatever they were, they didn't seem to like the light. Maybe that was significant? Maybe it wasn't? But it was all he had to work with.

Before setting off, earlier that day, Tony had insisted they bring a battery-powered lantern with them. It was the same one he and Joe used when they pitched their tent in the back garden as kids, but now Tony hung it from a tree branch behind him, in case one of the...Shadowmen, he had called them...tried to flank him. He had also managed to get the campfire going again by using the lining of his sleeping-bag as kindling.

With the lantern behind him, the flames in front and the torch being swung from left to right, Tony began to feel a little safer, but he could still see Shadowmen lurking in the trees. Some tried to edge forward, but only slowly. As they neared the lights, which Tony was now shrouded in, they shrieked and retreated back into the darkness.

Tony winced a little as his headache began to return. Just the stress of the situation, he thought to himself. Then his right arm jolted.

10

Charlie had marched along the poachers' trail for several hundred yards, the incline increasing as he made his way farther and farther up the embankment. His calves ached, making him wish he had spent as much time exercising his legs as his upper body when visiting the gym. The laughter continued up ahead. It was always up ahead; it never seemed to come any closer.

A few yards in front, just off the path, stood a wooden shack with a corrugated iron roof. The laughter seemed to be coming from inside it. Despite the cramp in his legs, Charlie ran up to it, confident he would find his tormentors hiding in there. He envisaged them huddling in the corner of the dwelling, sniggering at his expense. 'You'll be laughing on the other side of your faces in a minute,' Charlie grumbled.

As Charlie approached the shack, the smell of rotten wood seeped into his nose, the damp flooding his lungs. He coughed, covering his mouth with the back of his hand. There was a rectangular hole in the wood where a window had once been. Charlie peered in, shining the torch around the small room.

Mounted on the walls were rusted bear traps,

stuffed animal heads, aged rifles and other hunting paraphernalia. In the middle of the room was a small wooden table with animal bones scattered across it. Dirt now covered most of what had been a wooden floor, from which mushrooms and fungi now sprouted, spreading up the walls — but no people. Disappointed, Charlie turned back towards the path. Mike now stood in front of him.

At least, it was what remained of Mike. His skin was pale, with a greenish hint to it. There were deep wounds across his face and neck. Tears in his shirt revealed similar wounds across his chest. A gash across his forehead revealed bone.

'Forgetting somebody?' Mike asked. But his mouth did not move. The sound of his voice rang through Charlie's mind rather than being spoken aloud.

Mike lunged forward and took hold of Charlie's left forearm; the shock caused him to drop his torch and the bulb shattered as it hit the ground.

Mike's skin began to blister, the boils pulsating as pungent liquid seeped from the sores.

Charlie looked down at his arm, which Mike gripped tightly. The skin on Mike's hand burst into flames. Charlie looked up to find Mike's entire body was a raging inferno. Mike's flesh began to sizzle and fall away from the bone. Chunks of grilled meat fell to the ground. The heat caused fluids inside Mike's mole-like eyes to boil, and they exploded out of their sockets under the pressure. The smell of burning fat caused Charlie to retch. In the blink of an eye, all that remained was Mike's charred skeleton. A blackened skeletal hand now grasped Charlie's arm; its grip did not loosen.

Charlie blinked again and the skeleton was now gone, replaced by one of the shadowy entities they had previously encountered. The smell of burning now turned into the smell of sulphur. The grip round

Charlie's arm tightened, a vice clamping down upon his skin. His arm ached as flesh-numbing pains shot through it all the way up to his shoulder. He could now feel his skin beginning to stick to the inside of the creature's hand. He had felt this sensation once before, when he had placed the palm of his hand to the back of the freezer as part of a dare when he was twelve. He remembered how when he had pulled his hand away chunks of flesh were torn from his fingertips and remained stuck to the back of the ice-box.

Pulling his arm away, history repeated itself. Strips of flesh tore away from his wrists, the skin around the wounds blackened by frostbite. Charlie screamed in pain as he stumbled backward, stepping off the trail back towards the poachers' shack. The creature shrieked that ear-splitting scream. Several shadows of trees morphed into the elongated, humanoid shape of the creatures, which now lurked in the woods. Charlie turned and ran, his legs carrying him deeper into the darkness of the forest.

'Pigging hell! Pigging hell!' he whimpered as he swerved in and out of the trees. Not once did he turn to look behind him, but he could tell the creatures were gaining on him. The air grew colder and the smell of sulphur grew stronger. 'Pigging hell! Pigging hell!'

He was then halted by a sharp pain in his right leg, the bare leg, just above his ankle. He winced, telling himself it was cramp, and made another step forward. The pain grew stronger as something tightened round his calf, carving into the flesh. Charlie could feel warm blood running down his lower leg, soaking into his sock, the fabric sticking to the hairs on his shins.

Charlie looked down, squinting; something metallic was wrapped round his leg, glinting in the moonlight. He was caught in a snare.

He wriggled his leg in an attempt to shake the

snare loose, but this only caused it to tighten further. The brass wire now dug into the bone of his shin, but the adrenaline and fear, a fear of dying alone, prevented the intensity of the pain from increasing.

Shadows began to descend; the air tasted of frost and the smell, that smell of rotten eggs, grew stronger still. Charlie, his heart racing faster, beating stronger and stronger, lifted his right leg back then kicked forward as hard as he could. The wire snapped from its peg, the jolt caused Charlie to lose his balance, falling head-first, his arms extended in front to break his fall.

As he landed, Charlie's right hand connected with cold steel. In an instant there was click, then the sound of metal scraping against metal, as the rusted jaws of a bear trap slammed shut, its teeth crushing the bones in Charlie's wrist.

He broke out in a cold sweat, his entire body shaking. He began to vomit as the pain burned through his arm.

He attempted to pull his arm free; the metal teeth of the trap tore deeper through the tendons, tissue and bone of his wrist. He pulled again, this time with a twist, the bones cracking and breaking, the skin tearing. The smell of blood filled his nose; its metallic taste flooded his mouth. He vomited again, and his head span as he felt himself growing faint.

Something ice-cold scratched his wounded leg; a chill ran down his spine. Those things were now upon him, toying with him.

Grinding his teeth and gripping tightly onto the protruding root of a tree with his free hand, Charlie pulled and twisted his right arm. Bones cracked and broke further, the flesh tearing further. With a jolt his arm broke free. His hand, however, did not and was still in the grip of the trap. He screamed in terror as he stared at the stump where his hand had been severed from the wrist. A fountain of blood sprayed upward into his face. The stream shot up into his mouth, hitting the back of his throat, causing him to choke and splutter.

Charlie got to his feet, spitting the blood from his mouth, as one of the creatures was about to close its grip around his bloody ankle. With his only hand he grasped his right arm tightly in a vain attempt to stop the blood flow and began to limp frantically farther into the woods.

He stumbled and tripped into tree trunks, branches clawing his face. Something on the ground snapped underneath his feet — another trap. Something heavy swiftly moved through the treetops, branches snapping as it bulldozed its way through the canopy; autumn leaves rained down from their branches.

There was a swishing sound as a wooden pike swung down from the treetops, impaling Charlie, the spearhead penetrating his sternum and erupting from his spine. The force lifted him off his feet and then he slumped to his knees as it swung back like the pendulum of a grandfather clock. Charlie's lifeless head bobbed as the pike rocked gently, slowing to a stop.

The shadows released a disappointed groan and then retreated into the darkness.

11

At school the girl had once written a poem, using a lit candle as an analogy for the human spirit. She had described how brightly the candle shone for someone who led a fulfilled life, someone who was good-natured, strong-willed and kind to others. Someone, who when they died, would go to heaven. She then went on to write that when bad things happen, the flame becomes dimmer and the candle melts away. People who led a bad, unfulfilled life, with minimal willpower, had very little by way of an inner candle and unless they changed their life in order to make the flame burn brightly again, it would soon die altogether. All that would remain of their spirit would be a mound of wax and a blackened wick. She went on to write that these people would go to hell when they died.

Now she slept, still restrained to the roof of the cave. Her dreams were now more terrifying than ever and her subconscious kept recalling that poem and the image of a candle. Her candle — her soul.

In her earlier dreams the candle had been tall and thick and the flame burned bright, but slowly it began to melt and the flame slowly grew dimmer. There had been a brief moment where she sensed someone else was in the cave with her. Not her fiancé this time, but she certainly didn't feel alone. And in that moment the flame began to burn brightly again. But it wasn't to last long. Before she knew it she was alone again and the feeling of hopelessness returned, her light dimming.

In the dream she was now having, there was no candle, only a lump of wax, from which a wick sprouted. There was not much of a flame, more the glowing ember of the tip of the wick.

An icy, jet black hand with long, sharp fingers materialised in her dream. It floated over the remains of her candle then pinched the wick between its thumb and forefinger. With a faint hiss her light was gone.

12

Joe glanced at his watch; he had been hiking through the woods for roughly half an hour now with no sign of Mike. Luckily, he was yet to have another encounter with whoever or whatever they had met before.

Tony was convinced there was something unnatural, something supernatural, at play. But then, at least until the age of fourteen, Joe recalled, his brother had to sleep with the light on.

Joe was inclined to agree with Charlie, that it was nothing more than someone playing a prank. But if that was the case, who was behind it?

The only person who enjoyed a good prank or two was Charlie, but the whole thing was too elaborate for him to be able to pull off, especially as he was also on the receiving end of the joke. Apart from the people Joe had arrived in the woods with, the only other person who knew where he was this weekend was Linda. He considered whether or not she had a part to play in all this but felt guilty for believing the love of his life could be responsible for such a thing. He pushed the thought of Linda being involved out of his mind.

Joe pondered further possibilities and then he heard the screams again. They were spine-tingling and set him on edge. The cries appeared to be coming from a north-west direction, but with the woods being located in a valley, the sounds echoed in all directions. Practical joke or not, there was certainly something unnatural about those screams.

Joe now came to a clearing in the woods where a circle of stone tablets stood – the Druid Temple. In the centre of the circle was what appeared to be a stone table. The light from the full moon shone directly upon it. As Joe came closer to the stones, despite their weathered appearance, he could make out the runes carved into the ancient rock.

Joe was by no means a historian, but he had grown up in Raven's Peak and knew enough about the old stories of the druids who once worshiped in the woods centuries ago.

Stories of human sacrifice to pagan gods had become local legend. Recalling these stories now made Joe uneasy, given the night's events.

As Joe neared the stones he could see something laying on the table. He shone his torch upon it to reveal the corpse of a small animal. He leant in to see the lifeless creature had once been someone's pet cat. Its fur was black and matted with mud and dried blood. It had been placed on its back, its legs sprawled out; maggots squirmed from the cat's orifices, causing him to lift his hand to his mouth to stop him from vomiting. Encircling the dead cat were lumps of candlewax.

Joe lowered the torch and took a step back from the table. The beam of light caught something metallic hidden under the leaves, its reflection glinting in his eye. He bent down to for a closer inspection. Brushing away the dead leaves revealed a knife. It was no ordinary kitchen knife; it was some kind of antique dagger. Joe felt the weight of it; it was too heavy to be made of steel. If Joe was to take a guess he would have said it was made from iron. Similar runes to the ones carved into the stone table were also carved into the blade. The blade was also stained with blood. Had someone sacrificed poor Tiddles to an ancient god? Joe laughed at the idea and how stupid it had sounded.

He placed the knife on the table and the moment he pulled his hand back music began to play. The song radiated from his pocket, which began to vibrate wildly. His phone was ringing; the unexpectedness caused him to jump back. He shook his head, disappointed in his reaction. Joe pulled the phone from his pocket and glanced at the screen which read: Tony calling.

Joe accepted the call and placed the phone to his ear. The sound of static and interference drowned out Tony's voice as the line kept cutting out.

'Tony... Tony? What's... I can't hear you. Say it again —'

The phone beeped twice and then the call cut out completely. Joe cussed at the phone, thrust it back into his pocket and raced back to the campsite.

***

The fire was now slowly dying; the flames consumed the last of the wood. The lantern, which hung from the tree, now began to flicker. As the shield of light began to dull, the Shadowmen edged forwards a few yards closer to Tony.

To make matters worse, his head still throbbed and his convulsions had not settled.

13

Joe sprinted through the woods, a look of determination on his face, gritting his teeth as he ran. The beam of light darted back and forth as he carried the torch in his left hand. Something clawed his right-hand side, the wound numb with cold. Joe brought himself to a stop and pivoted to the right. A shadow darted back into the cover of the trees as he shone the torch around, looking for the attacker.

A chill grew in the air and vapour escaped from Joe's lips. He was now aware of something behind him. The smell of burned matches lingered. Joe stood still, not daring to turn round. His side throbbed as frost nipped at his skin.

Joe prepared to run when a cold grip wrapped round his ankles. His legs were pulled out from beneath him, making him drop his torch as he tumbled face-first towards the dirt. The torch, still lit, hit the ground and rolled underneath a nearby briar bush.

Fingers gripped Joe's shoulder and he was flipped forcefully over onto his back. The impact of his spine connecting with the ground knocked the wind out of him. He gasped as the entity, like the ones his party had encountered before, glided across his body.

While the silhouette was humanoid in shape, there

was no depth. It was as thin as paper, its shape filling the contours of his body like a shroud. In Joe's eyes it was no more than a shadow being cast over him. But the shadow had weight and strength. A scream rose from its featureless face.

Now face to face with Joe, it paused for a brief moment, then its head bobbed up and down, as if to size up whether its catch was worth keeping or throwing back. It screamed again, only this time there appeared to be excitement in the tone. Then the shrieks became short and sharp, almost rhythmic. Joe sensed it was calling for more of its kind. Joe kept his entire body still, with the exception of his right hand, which now frantically searched the forest floor for anything he could use as a weapon.

The creature ran its claws across Joe's face, its fore and index fingers ploughing the skin from the corner of his right eye, down his cheek to his jaw; the wounds frosted over. His hand, still scrambling for a defence, now swung underneath the briar patch.

The creature's fingers, while freezing, were smooth like obsidian and now slid down Joe's neck — only now the cuts were less shallow. The movement of the fingertips seemed to intentionally avoid any major veins or arteries. It certainly didn't want its prey to bleed-out.

Its clawed hand paused over Joe's chest. It could feel the strong, rhythmic pounding of his heart. Another excited scream rose from its blank face and then it dug its claws deep into the flesh and muscle of Joe's torso, tearing through his shirt. Blood oozed from the wounds, matting the hair of his chest. Joe grimaced, his eyelids tightly closed, bravely holding back the scream. If he screamed he would be admitting defeat.

Dark fingers buried deeper into Joe's chest; cold radiated from the tips, sending bitter shockwaves through his body. Joe shuddered as the chill ran down his spine to his core. Yet, his right hand did not give up its search.

As Joe's hand scrambled under the brambles, the thorns raked the skin on the back of his hand and his fingers, peeling back the cuticles. Then the edge of his palm brushed against something solid and heavy. The object rolled away slightly then rolled back. Joe took hold of it with a tight grip. It was smooth, with a rubbery texture. It was his torch.

The moment his fingers wrapped round the grip of the torch Joe's world slowed to a crawl, when in the real world the following sequence of events unfolded in a matter of seconds.

He took an underhand grip on the torch and lifted it up through the brambles, bringing it back down towards the creature's head in a stabbing motion, the light still shining bright. Before the torch could connect with the creature, its heavenly beam shone upon the top of the jet black, featureless head. The creature released one of its high-pitched, ear-piercing wails. But this time, it was a scream of pain. Smoke began to smoulder from the area that would have an eye. It jolted its head back, avoiding a blow from the torch.

Joe made a backhand swing with the torch, the light cutting through the creature's neck like a surgical laser. The creature screamed as its head slipped away from its neck; smoke escaped from it shoulders. The severed head still emitted the howl as it dropped to the ground and, as it fell, Joe saw the blackness of the thing that had almost beaten him now began to turn a shade of grey. The creature's body now froze, changing to the same grey colour as its head had done. It now looked statuesque in appearance, like it had caught a glimpse of Medusa. And then the creature exploded into a cloud of ash, which was carried away in the breeze like burnt paper.

Joe brought himself to his knees; his world now sped back up to its normal pace. He coughed as he inhaled the smoke and ash that lingered in the air. Shakily he now got to his feet and as he did several more of the creatures materialised from the shadows. They hissed at Joe, who stood now, holding the grip of the torch in both hands like he was holding onto a baseball bat, the beam shone over his right shoulder and into the night sky.

The creatures screamed in unison; every muscle in Joe's body was tense and the adrenaline overflowed, surging through his veins. He trembled but his heart beat with courage gained from the knowledge that these monsters could be hurt and, from what he had witnessed, even killed.

The shadowy pack stood still, holding their ground. Joe held his, his instincts now at loggerheads. Should he take flight or should he fight? The creatures screamed once more. Joe licked the blood that had pooled at the corner of his mouth as it had run down his cheek. The creatures began to edge forward. Joe tightened the grip on the torch and snarled. 'Come at me!' he roared.

14

Tony leapt into his tent as the fire began to die. The batteries of the lantern had bitten the dust sometime earlier.

He now sat cross-legged in the middle of the tent. His head still hurt and his shoulders and arms still convulsed. The shadows danced round the tent, calling his name, but for now his torch protected him. Afraid of the light, the Shadowmen stayed on the outside.

Tony tried to contact his brother again. His hand shaking, he pulled the phone from his pocket and dialled the number. The phone beeped twice and the display told him the connection had failed.

He now heard the Shadowmen scream, followed by shouting and a lot of commotion. Tony had the urge to see what was happening outside, but he stayed put in the safety of the tent.

Joe tore into the campsite, swinging the torch left to right, as if he were wielding a battle axe; the creatures screaming at him. Some of them tried to attack but were met by the beam of light from his torch, transforming them into a statue before they exploded into a cloud of ash. Others flittered in and out of the shadows to avoid the offense. Those that remained soon made a retreat into the darkness of the woods. But Joe knew that sooner or later they would return in force.

He looked around for a moment, but neither his brother nor his friends were anywhere to be seen. Then he saw a faint glow from Tony's tent. Without any consideration for the zip, he ripped open the door of the tent. Relief washed over him the moment he saw his brother sat in the middle.

Tony looked up. 'Are they gone?'

'Yeah, they're gone — for now. You can come out,' Joe said.

Tony crawled out of the tent, stood up and hugged his brother. He smiled for a brief moment then his eyes rolled back and his body stiffened, falling backwards. Joe managed to catch him before his head hit the ground. Tony's entire body began to convulse, his arms and legs flailing; the colour ran from his cheeks and a blue tinge appeared in his lips as he wet himself.

Joe laid his brother gently on the ground, cushioning his head with a rolled up sleeping bag. The instructions their mother had given them as children now came flooding back. How long had it been since Tony last had a seizure? Five or ten years? Joe could not recall, as he now rolled his brother over into the recovery position. Once his brother was settled, Joe strategically positioned their torches so that two beams of light shone directly on them.

The shadowy creatures watched curiously from the treeline. This compassionate behaviour intrigued them, but they dared not approach any closer for fear of the light.

After several minutes Tony slowly began to regain consciousness. He tried to speak, but could only manage a croak.

'Take it easy,' Joe whispered.

Tony cleared his throat and tried again. 'What happened?'

'You had a fit,' Joe answered outright. 'I've not seen you have one of those in years.'

'Twelve,' Tony muttered.

'Come again?'

'I was twelve the last time I had a seizure.'

He paused as the warm dampness of his pants now registered with him. The colour in his cheeks came rushing back, the paleness replaced by the glow of embarrassment. 'I pissed myself, didn't I?' he moaned with shame.

Joe chuckled. 'Yeah, afraid so. Don't worry, I won't tell the others.'

Tony slowly propped himself up on one elbow. 'Have you seen them?'

Joe shook his head. 'Nope. I'm guessing they didn't make it back here then.'

'I think the Shadowmen have them.'

'The what-men?'

'The Shadowmen. It's what I named those things out there in the woods.'

Joe smiled; his brother, now twenty-four, still maintained a childlike innocence about him. It gave him comfort. 'Well, that's as good a name as any, I guess.' Joe paused for a moment. 'And, I even think we can kill these Shadowmen.'

Tony sat up. His eyes widened as Joe spoke about his encounter near the monoliths. He concluded by saying, 'So, light appears to be the key, as far as I can tell.'

Joe rummaged in one of the backpacks and pulled out two unopened bottles of water. He threw one over to Tony and kept the other for himself. He removed the cap, guzzled about half of the bottle in a single breath and then wiped his mouth with the back of his hand.

'And then there is this...' Joe said as he lifted up his

shirt; dried blood had glued the fabric to his chest. He winced as he pulled the shirt away, tearing hair from his chest.

Tony examined the wound.

'On my face too,' said Joe, turning his head. The wounds on his face and chest had stopped bleeding, but the cuts themselves were blackened. The skin around each cut was red-raw from cold.

'That looks like frostbite,' Tony ventured.

Joe lowered his shirt. 'It was freezing cold. When it touched me it felt like ice. And it stank. It had a similar smell to burning matches...' He paused a moment. 'Worse, it was almost like rotten eggs.'

Tony sighed. 'I might sound crazy, but I really don't think they are human. I don't even think they are animals. They are something completely different.'

Joe nodded in agreement. 'Whatever they are, they're not natural.'

Tony looked round, trying to make out shadows past the trees. 'I think they have gone, for now, but I can't tell if I'm looking at the shadows of the trees or if it's them.'

'If they are there the light is keeping them away for now,'

'That won't last long though, the batteries will soon die. We need to get out of here — go get help!' Tony said with urgency.

Joe pondered the situation for a moment, 'Mike and Charlie could still be out there, and we need to find them. I can't leave a man behind.'

Tony protested. Occasions where Tony stood up to his brother were very few and far between but getting to safety seemed a greater priority than finding their friends, and so he spoke up. 'You can't leave a man behind? Joe, this isn't a war and you're not a soldier. You never have been. I know you have such loyalty to your friends and I love you for it, but what about the loyalty to your own brother?' He stopped, expecting a comeback, but there was none and so he continued. 'We can go get the police, bring them back here and they can look.'

Joe shook his head then stood up, pacing round the camp. 'And tell the police what exactly?' He ignored the soldier comment. 'We tell them the Shadowmen took them? They wouldn't believe us.' He stretched out his arms, interlocking his fingers to crack his knuckles, glancing at his watch as he drew his arms back.

Joe stood up and looked directly at Tony. 'The sun will be up in two hours or so. When it does I think these things will go into hiding or risk being turned to dust. These things, they hide within the dark places, in the daytime I don't think they will be much bother. We can hold out here till then and once the sun is up we'll spend a few hours looking for Mike and Charlie. If we don't find them by —' he glanced at his watch again '— say ten am, then we'll go get help.'

Tony let out a long sigh and reluctantly agreed. For the next ten minutes not a word was spoken.

Tony took a deep breath, knees trembling as he prepared to tell his brother what had been bothering him since yesterday. He was afraid of how his confession would hurt Joe, but he was afraid of not leaving the woods alive even more so. He didn't want to die with guilt on his conscience and now seemed as good a time as any. There might not be another chance.

'Joe, I need to tell you something...' he began, but as he spoke the light from his torch began to flicker and fade.

15

The moment Tony's torch died, the Shadowmen reappeared. They did not travel through the trees or along the trails, they simply materialised up from the shadows.

The most Joe could account for were ten Shadowmen. Each stood in the shadows of the trees, shadows of rock formations, shadows of the tents, even Joe and Tony's own shadows. The Shadowmen stood where the light could not fall; within the dark places, as Joe had noted.

Tony's instinct was to bolt like a frightened rabbit. He took a step forward but Joe pulled him back, his eyes wild, filled with anger. Tony had seen this look on his brother before. It was the look on his face when he competed in his races, a look he only wore when he was losing.

'I'm fed up of running,' Joe said, one hand still on Tony's shoulder, his eyes on the shadows.

Joe was now aware the Shadowmen had increased in number and formed a circle round them. The air grew cold and there was a potent smell of sulphur. Joe pulled his little brother closer to him and swung his torch in all directions. Some of the Shadowmen disappeared then resurrected from another shadow to dodge the torch's beam. Others were hit with the spotlight and exploded into a cloud of dust.

Tony began to whimper.

'Use your phone, the flash from your camera-phone!' Joe screamed. Tony did as he was ordered; he pulled the phone from his pocket, opened the camera application and began snapping wildly. The light was not strong enough to destroy the creatures, but they thought twice before making an assault. This gave Tony confidence and without realising it he was now moving away from his brother, standing his own ground.

The phone beeped as a warning flashed across the screen to indicate the battery was low. The excessive use of the camera had drained its power severely. The phone then shut itself down and switched off.

Tony screamed for help as a swarm of shadows glided towards him, clawed hands reaching out. Joe was caught in his own battle; surrounded, he swung the torch erratically, unable to come to his brother's aid. Thinking quickly, he withdrew his own phone from his pocket and tossed it to his brother. Tony fumbled the catch and dropped the phone. The screen cracked as it landed on a rock. The impact caused the casing to come loose and the battery was flung into the undergrowth.

Tony picked up the body of the phone and made a dive towards the spot where he had seen the battery land, hoping it would still work if he was able to piece it back together. He belly flopped to the ground, winded. Then something cold took hold of his ankles and began to pull him back. He tried to scream for his brother, but as his breath had not returned to him no sound was produced.

The horde which surrounded Joe had almost been dispersed. Those who had not been turned to dust were flitting in and out of the shadows to evade attack. Joe turned to his brother to find him being dragged into the shadows of the woods, his fingers raking up dirt, dead leaves and twigs as he was pulled into the darkness. Joe began to give chase, lifting his high-powered torch, shining it directly on Tony, but as he did more Shadowmen materialised in his path to form a blockade, taking a direct hit from the light. They exploded almost instantly, leaving behind a cloud of dust and ash which seeped into Joe's lungs and stung his eyes. He coughed uncontrollably and dropped the torch, which switched off as it hit the ground. Joe rubbed his eyes; tears welled up and streamed down his face. He stumbled around, unable to see, unaware that he had kicked the torch and sent it rolling farther ahead.

Joe's vision soon returned to normal and when he gained control of his breathing he ran towards where the torch now lay.

A shadow cast by a tree lay across his path; from it materialised three Shadowmen. They screamed in unison as they formed a barricade in front of the torch. Joe gritted his teeth as the soundwave penetrated his ear.

Another group of Shadowmen began to emerge from the darkness of the trees to his right and then another band to his left.

Joe stood on the spot, his body still, only his eyes moving as they flicked left to right, looking for a way round the blockade. There was none. He clenched his fists, angry at the prospect of going back on his earlier protest to stand and fight. A protest which he now considered could have resulted in his brother's death. The brother he had always sworn to protect.

The shadows moved in closer, beginning to trap Joe in a pincer. Joe muttered several curse words under his breath, span round 180 degrees and ran.

16

Joe made a mad dash to the east; his sprint, under different circumstances, would have beaten his personal best. His feet pounded the ground as he ran, kicking up clouds of dirt that fogged around his ankles, his heart hammering hard. As he made his escape something crunched under his boot. It was one of the fireworks that had been scattered around the outskirts of the campsite. Joe paid it no attention and continued running.

He was now heading back in the direction of the ancient monument, but this time along a different path to the one he had taken before. This area of the woods was the densest part of the forest. To his left a steep embankment was eroded into the hillside. Without the aid of his torch or any other light source, he was almost in total darkness and in danger of dropping off the edge.

Joe ran blindly though the trees, squinting to see what was in front of him. It did little to help; branches scratched at his face, arms and legs, his shins grazing tree stumps, his ankles smashing into rocks, but he kept on running.

A stitch rapidly formed in his side. The pain was searing but Joe pushed on, his legs tiring. He had no plan other than to keep running until he cleared the woods and reached one of the surrounding meadows. Perhaps the open space would offer little shadow for the dark creatures to hide.

Despite the heat that now flushed through Joe's body, he could feel a frigid breeze over his back; they were gaining on him. He now began to lose his pace as the terror of being lost to the shadows began to flow through him. Tiring, he now stumbled and tripped his way through the trees, catching branches to break his fall. And then he made a mistake, which any experienced runner should know to avoid, which in any other situation he knew himself well enough to avoid. A schoolboy error: he turned his head to look behind him. This caused him to lose focus, being less aware of his surroundings. He turned his head forward again but he did not react quick enough to avoid the wide trunk of an oak tree, which stood directly in his path.

Joe hit the trunk hard, the bark of the tree leaving an imprint across his face. Blood streamed from his nose. But, he was still on his feet. In a daze he staggered back and forth and then he felt his weight fall backward. He took a few steps back to regain his balance, but with his head spinning he had no consciousness of his surroundings. His foot slipped over the edge of the embankment, and the rest of his body followed.

Joe tumbled head over heels, his body smashing against rocks and tree branches as he bounced down embankment. Rolling six feet, twelve feet, twenty-four feet. Then he hit the ground hard as he reached the foot of the hill, the back of his head colliding with a boulder.

He lay still, staring up through the tree canopy towards the stars, watching the world spin. A troop of Shadowmen encroached into his field of vision and then there was only darkness.

17

The girl, hands still bound, became aware that once more there was someone else in the cave with her. Although her eyes had no more adjusted to the light than when she had first found herself in such surroundings, she could sense the presence of somebody else, different to the malevolent force that had been with her previously — someone human. But, her awareness was only instinct. Twenty-four hours ago the prospect of someone else entering the cave would have filled her with optimism, a hope of being rescued, but now, other than a primal awareness, their presence did not even register with her. She was awake, for all intents and purposes, but devoid of any higher consciousness, empty of any freewill.

**

Tony began to dream a very vivid, unpleasant dream.

Within his dream he recalled a memory of an event that had only occurred within the last few days. A memory that caused him a great discomfort, a secret he harboured, afraid of the consequences if it was set free.

The weekend before the camping trip, Joe's fiancée, Linda, invited Tony to join them for a home cooked meal. Tony jumped at the chance — he adored Linda's cooking. The evening was a success, the sense of family ever-present.

Joe's job as an electrician for the local council often meant he would be called upon at a minute's notice. If a set of traffic lights failed, the council would call Joe. If a power line went down, they'd call Joe. This particular night, Joe received such a call. He quickly changed his clothes, kissed Linda and left, leaving his fiancée and brother to finish their supper.

Alone, Linda suggested they retreat to the living room to finish their drinks. By this time Tony was a little intoxicated. He had never been a drinker (for fear it would trigger a seizure), only having a tipple every now and then, and even the slightest drop of alcohol went straight to his head.

They had sat on the couch and Tony admired Linda's beauty. His eyes glanced over her light blonde bobbed hair, her green eyes, and her slim, athletic body. He'd wanted to kiss her — had wanted to since the moment Joe had introduced her. With his inhibitions quietened by the alcohol, he did.

At first, under the influences of the bottle of wine she had consumed with dinner, Linda had returned the kiss. All too quickly she had come to her senses and gently pushed Tony away. He'd apologised, blaming his advances on the drink, and she accepted, explaining it was only a drunken accident, water under the bridge — certainly not worth dwelling on. To Tony, however, kissing the fiancée of a brother who had always been there for him, who had always protected him and helped to raise him, this was the ultimate betrayal. This feeling of guilt had been slowly eating away at him ever since.

But this wasn't the only secret Tony had kept from his brother. In truth, despite everything Joe had done for him, Tony was jealous.

He was jealous of Joe's handsome, athletic looks. He was jealous of Joe's demeanour and good nature. He was jealous of Joe's popularity – especially with the ladies. He was especially jealous of the relationship his brother had with Linda. But more so, he was jealous of how his mother had treated her eldest son; giving him the freedom to live his life. And now, as he dreamed, this jealously turned to anger and hate.

Tony, as he continued to dream, now found himself stood in the centre of an underground carpark. Lights stretched the breadth and width of the garage, buzzing overhead, blinding. The temperature now began to drop, almost to freezing point. Tony thrust his hands under his armpits to try and keep warm, shivering as he did so, vapour escaping from his lips as he exhaled. But the drop in temperature did little to cool the jealous rage that was now all-consuming. From behind him, he heard familiar laughter. He spun round and saw his brother and his fiancée, their arms wrapped round each other's waists. Tony realised that they weren't just laughing with each other, they were laughing at him, muttering words such 'loser', 'pathetic' and 'Mummy's boy' under their breaths.

Tony's hands dropped to his sides, his fists clenched. 'Stop it!' he shouted. 'Stop talking about me!' They disappeared. In their place stood a Shadowman and next to it a light-switch materialised on the wall.

The rage continued to boil uncontrollably inside Tony. And then he burst, an angry confession split from him. 'I hate you! I always have! You had it all and I was left with nothing.' A part of Tony knew this wasn't true but he couldn't hold his anger back. It felt as though the Shadowman was coaxing the confession from him.

'Well I've tasted what you taste.' He gritted his teeth, clenched his fists and screwed up his eyes, trying to hold in the next thought. His whole body began to quiver as he couldn't hold back any longer. 'I kissed Linda!' he screamed, the sound tearing his throat as the words broke free from within him.

The moment the words left Tony's mouth, the black hand of the Shadowman rose up and flicked the light-switch. On either side of the carpark the lights switched off, from the outer edge, working inward. Each light went out with a bang, glass shattering, pouring down upon the tarmac, the explosion echoed from wall to wall. The speed at which the lights extinguished accelerated, an inescapable darkness swept in from all angles. Tony stood staring up at the spotlight of the last light which shone upon him. Then it died.

Tony now stood in total darkness. A darkness which he could not escape from — all consuming.

18

Joe woke abruptly, taking in a sharp lungful of air, the force of which burned the back of throat. At the same time a sharp pain fluctuated through his lower ribs on his right hand side; they were undoubtedly cracked from the tumble he had taken. It was this pain which had pulled Joe from the nightmare he was having, a dream which now eluded him. A pain which reminded him he was still alive.

Although his eyes were wide open, he could not see — not through blindness but due to the lack of light in the new surroundings. Joe winced as his side throbbed; a similar pain also ran across the bridge of his nose and a dull, tired ache ran through his arms. He now realised his arms were held above his head, something coarse wrapped round his wrists. He tried to lower his arms but they were bound to something above.

He closed his eyes in an attempt to gain focus; the smell of damp infiltrated his nostrils. He stretched his fingers and could feel the rugged surface of rock above him; the sound of dripping water echoed. Considering the limited information he had gained, Joe concluded he was in a cave of sorts, somewhere underground.

Deprived of visual aids, he tried to utilise his other senses. The cave offered nothing new in terms of smells, but he could hear the sound of breathing only several feet from him. Relief washed over him as he realised he was not alone. 'Tony, is that you?' There was no response. He then heard the breathing of a second person. 'Mike?' he called. 'Charlie?' The only reply was his own voice being echoed around the cave.

Joe wriggled his hands, feeling the restraints with the heel of his palms. They felt natural, almost plant-like in texture. Joe was no botanist by any means, but if he would hazard a guess he would say the restraints were made from vines. He felt round further with his fingertips and ascertained the vines were rooted into the roof of the cave. He attempted to pull his arms lose, but the pain in his ribs escalated. 'Son of...!' he growled. He composed himself for a moment then tried again. The pain worsened, causing him to cry out again. 'C'mon, c'mon,' he muttered, psyching himself up for another attempt. Then he yanked his arms with all his strength and the vine broke away from the cave roof with a snap. The pain in Joe's ribs was excruciating, intensifying further from the impact of hitting the ground, landing on his injured side. He screamed, tears swelling in his eyes.

Once he had composed himself he rolled onto his front, leading with his good side. As he did an object inside his pocket dug into his leg. It was the Zippo lighter. He brought himself to his feet and took the light from his pocket, igniting it; the smell of gasoline was intoxicating.

The glow of the orange flame was pitiful in the darkness of the cave, but it was just enough to allow Joe to see arm's length in front of him. He took two steps forward and the flame revealed the shape of someone else suspended from the roof of the cave. It was Tony.

Joe lifted the lighter closer to Tony's face. He was unconscious, his head slumped, his chin resting on his collar bone, but other than some icy burns across his chest he appeared to be in good shape.

Joe flicked the lighter off and placed it back in his pocket in order to free both hands. He reached up and fumbled round in the darkness in an effort to release Tony's restraints. Although the pain still radiated through Joe's ribs he persisted in freeing his brother. After a few moments Joe managed to tear through the vines, causing Tony to drop to the ground. Joe retrieved the lighter and sparked the flame once more. He pulled the remnants of the vines from Tony's wrists and began to slap his cheeks gently, calling his name. He did not respond. However, he generally appeared to be okay, and as there was no immediate danger, Joe then turned to search for the other person he could hear breathing in the cave.

He took a few steps forward, the lighter held out in front of him at arm's length; he was adamant he would be reunited with Mike or Charlie. Joe lurched forward and the image of a scantily-clad young woman came into view.

He holstered the lighter and began to untie her restraints; as he did she released a faint groan, which was at least more of a response than he received from his brother. Joe gently lowered her to the ground, supporting her head. 'Hey, are you okay?' Joe whispered. She groaned again. 'Can you hear me?' he asked urgently. The question was answered with a grunt. He made use of the lighter once more, the glow revealing the girl was awake, a vacant expression in her eyes. 'What's your name? How did you get here?' he enquired. The girl's eyes closed and her head fell back. Joe shook her. 'Hey, stay with me.' She lifted her head and opened her eyes, the vacant expression still there. 'What's your name?' Joe persisted.

'D-D-Dan...' Her speech slurred into silence.

'Danielle?'

The girl grunted.

'Danielle?' There was no response, but this name was as good as any. 'Danielle, I need to check on my brother, he's lying over there, but I'll be straight back. I promise.' The only response from Danielle was another moan.

He hopped over to his brother and crouched down next to him. 'Tony, come on, bro', we need to go.' He continued to tap his brother's cheek but there was still no response. 'Tony, come on. We need to find a way out of here. Now!' Tony began to cough and splutter. Joe smiled with relief as his brother began to catch his breath. The coughing continued, becoming more violent, projecting a sticky fluid into Joe's face. He wiped his face clean with his hand and proceeded to examine the substance which had accumulated on his fingertips. It was viscous, like phlegm in texture, but jet black in colour. Then Tony's entire body began to convulse.

With all four of his brother's limbs in spasm, Joe leaned back to avoid taking a fist to the jaw. Then Tony's body stiffened and his eyes sprang open; black tears shed and rolled down his face, leaving oily marks across his cheeks. 'Tony?' Joe whispered, as he placed his free hand on his brother's forehead. His skin was hot to the touch and began to blister. In that moment, his entire body burst into flames; a state of spontaneous combustion.

Joe leaped backward, tripping over Danielle's legs. He landed on his back, dropping the lighter. The flames from his brother's body then died and the cave plunged into darkness.

Joe fumbled round for the lighter while crying out for his brother. His fingers connected with metal and he gripped the object tightly. The dull orange light came to life once more and Joe cautiously approached the spot where his brother had been, only instead of the scorched remains of a human body he had expected, there stood a Shadowman.

Leading with the lighter, Joe lunged at it, cursing. 'Where's my brother?!' he demanded. 'What did you do to him?!' The flame was not strong enough to hurt the creature like the intense light of the torch had done to the others, but it was still cautious. It edged back slowly. Joe brought the flame nearer to its featureless face. The shadow screamed that high-pitched howl the creatures emitted and disappeared into the dark recesses of the cave. Joe gave chase but it was gone. The smell of sulphur lingered. Joe may have lost the creature, but what he did find was the start of a tunnel.

19

Beyond the cave led a network of tunnels. Joe had no idea where he was going but he soldiered on regardless.

Joe's mind replayed the events in the cave — one minute Tony was there, then the flames and then he was gone with a Shadowman in his place. Joe didn't believe his brother was dead; there was no body. Maybe Tony wasn't in the cave after all and it was some trick of the mind which these creatures were playing. But if that was the case, why was Joe seeing Danielle? If she was an illusion, why had his mind conceived her?

Danielle limped alongside him, his arm was wrapped round her waist, her own slung over his shoulder for support. Periodically Joe would ask his companion if she was okay, if she was hanging in there, but only monosyllabic grunts and groans escaped her lips.

The caves and tunnels were eerily quiet. There was no sign of the demonic shadows that had plagued both Joe and Danielle; the only sound was the echo of drops of water hitting the ground.

There was something ominous about the sudden disappearance of these Shadowmen. Joe felt the spirits were lying in wait, ready to ambush him round the next corner. He didn't want to hang around to find out.

After blindly wandering in the dark for the best part of an hour, Joe began to feel a light draught on his cheek. He jumped; his heart felt as if it had burst from his chest. His gut instinct told him it was the shadowy spirits, but, although cool, the breeze was not glacial like the air had been when in their presence.

Joe glanced round for any sign of the creatures, but there did not appear to be any immediate danger. He raised his hand to feel the breeze growing stronger and then headed in the direction it was blowing from, dragging Danielle along with him. He grew excited at the prospect of a way out, but she did not share this enthusiasm, only remaining her non-responsive self.

The breeze led the pair into a large chamber. A foot above Joe's head, moonlight shone through a crack in the cave wall. He slowly let go of Danielle, making sure she was steady on her feet before going to inspect the potential escape route.

Reaching up, he tapped his knuckles around the fracture in the wall. It made a dull hollow sound. The texture of the cave felt different here, like masonry plaster rather than stone. Joe drew back a clenched fist and, closing his eyes to brace himself, he prepared to punch the cave ceiling. He took a deep breath and let his fist fly.

His hand broke through with ease and the cool night air kissed his knuckles. He opened his eyes and laughed manically with triumph. He felt the outside world, his fingertips touching soft dirt, wet grass and damp leaves; they were at least seven feet underground. 'There's a way out!' He turned to Danielle, but she was still in her dreamlike state.

Joe pulled at the cave wall, tearing a hole large enough for him to climb through; the moonlight illuminated the cave. He ran to Danielle and dragged her by her arm over to their exit. The pain in his ribs had by no means disappeared, but the adrenaline that now flowed through his body from the prospect of being free from the catacombs made it easier to bear.

He lifted Danielle by her waist and she instinctively reached for the hole, not being consciously aware of her actions. She pushed her arms through the gap and dug her fingers into the earth to pull herself up. Joe switched the position of his hands and pushed her up from her buttocks. Joe watched her escape into the silvery light of the moon and then he proceeded to climb out.

Joe got to his feet and looked round. They were standing in the centre of the circle of druid stones; they had broken out through the underside of the stone table.

Joe paced back and forth trying to get his bearings, formulating some kind of a plan. He turned his head east, the horizon was now a dark shade of blue, rather than the black night that was directly overhead; the sun was beginning to rise.

'Okay, here's what we're going to do,' he said, almost to himself. 'My car is just on the other side of the woods; we're going to run as quick as we can to it. I'm going to take you back into town. The sun will be up soon, so once you're safe I'm going to come back and look for my brother and my friends.'

Danielle muttered something under her breath as she stared up at the moon. Joe couldn't make out what she said; it just sounded like another incoherent moan. If he had been closer to her, he may have heard her say, 'No use, they're with us now. Soon you'll be with us too.'

The temperature in the air dropped and the smell of burnt matches was carried on the wind. The branches of the trees began to shakes and rustle, casting their leaves from them as a thick black cloud of smoke seeped through the canopy. A frostbitten wind howled, blowing through their hair and making their clothes flutter. The moonlight began to disappear, blocked out by the mass of clouds. The Shadowmen were swarming upon them.

20

Quickly, Joe broke off a length of tree branch and tore the sleeve away from his shirt, which he then wrapped round the end of the bough. He lit the fabric and prayed the torched would not burn itself out too soon. He grabbed Danielle by her upper arm and dragged her into the trees. She ran with no real awareness of her actions, simply following his lead.

The swarm descended and a wave of frost formed on the ground where it had passed over.

They now reached the ravine, which Joe had fallen foul to earlier. Not wanting to repeat this error, he slowed down to a brisk walk, hoping the flame from the torch would be sufficient to ward off the evil that pursued them.

Joe glanced over his shoulder; the swarm was now at their heels. Joe flung Danielle in front and began to push her along the trail as he began to run again. A blanket of black smoke now engulfed the pair, frost savagely biting the parts of their bodies that were bare. The torch, however, appeared to be doing its job. Apart from the severe cold from the sheer number of shadows, they appeared to be too cautious of the light of the flame to physically touch Joe or Danielle.

The swarm now flew past them and ascended up

through the trees, above the canopy of the forest.

The campsite now came into view as the foliage became less dense. The swarm of Shadowmen now turned and descended back down towards them. Joe's foot caught a protruding tree root and he tumbled to the ground. By some miracle he managed to keep hold the torch despite hitting the ground side on, his cracked ribs connecting with the solid earth. The moment Joe released his grip from Danielle she stopped dead in her tracks.

Joe rolled on the ground in agony, but kept his grasp on the torch. 'Keeping going!' he yelled at Danielle, as the swarm now crashed through the leaves above. 'Go!' he yelled. 'That way!' He pointed in the direction of the meadow he and his friends had crossed to reach the woods. The moment Joe gave the command, Danielle obeyed without question. She staggered through the trees, but Joe's sight of her was blocked as the shadows swarmed upon him.

The shadows now engulfed him, but the flame of the torch still held them off. Joe tightly closed his eyes, grimacing, as the bitter winds blew through his hair and over his body as the smoke passed over. The breeze from the last of the swarm blew out the torch.

Joe dropped the scorched branch and rolled onto his back. Through the trees he could see a black nimbus forming as the swarm gathered once more. This time, however, they did not descend straight away. The shadow-cloud now took on a humanoid shape: one gigantic Shadowman made up of hundreds.

Joe tried to pick himself up but the pain was too intense. The best he could manage was to crawl on his back towards the campsite. As his legs pushed the rest of his body through the mud, the gigantic Shadowman began to speak as it lingered above the tree tops. The voice was a chorus of hundreds of individual voices, a collective all talking in unison which echoed across the valley. A voice which was unmistakably female.

'You, mortal, have disturbed our slumber.'

Joe continued crawling on his back.

'You, mortal, have vanquished many of our brothers and sisters, but you will not see the light of day.'

Something now dug into Joe's back as he crawled into the perimeter of the campsite. He reached underneath him and pulled out the object; it was an extremely large and powerful firework. Scattered around him were several smaller fireworks. The titanic Shadowman continued to speak.

'For we are darkness. We are many. We are legion.'

Still sprawled on the ground, Joe gathered up the fireworks and pegged them into the dirt. He withdrew the lighter from his pocket and flipped the lid. The swarm, holding its shape of a single Shadowman, was now directly overhead. Joe lit the fuse on largest firework first and then lit the rest. The voice continued to echo.

'We shall purge the flesh from your bones and devour your soul...' The last syllable pronounced in a high-pitched shrill.

Joe snarled as the fuses burnt away. 'Devour this, bitch!'

A volley of bright white balls of fire shot out from the largest firework with a screech which was on par with the cry of the Shadowmen, and then it disappeared into the body of the swarm. The smaller fireworks followed suit. There was a rally of blinding flashes followed by a multitude of explosions; Druid Wood fell into a multicolour blitz.

The swarm of shadows screamed in pain, as various coloured flashes erupted like rainbow lightening under the dark vapour. There were further screams and then the cloud dispersed. Ash began to rain down upon the trees below.

Joe lay on his back staring up at the stars, smiling as the firework display drew to a close. He always had enjoyed a good firework show.

21

Joe limped out of the woods, clutching his side, his clothes and hair greyed by dust and ash. Standing still at the far end of the meadow he saw Danielle.

When Joe reached her he placed a hand on her shoulder and smiled. 'I think we're safe now.' She did not respond — she didn't even appear to acknowledge him. She must be in a deep state of shock, Joe thought, some kind of trauma. He smiled at Danielle again. 'I'll get you to a hospital. When we get into town is there any one you want me to call. A friend? A boyfriend? Family?' His voice was slower and louder than usual, as if he were talking to someone who was hard of hearing, but her vacant expression remained. Joe gave her another smile and, taking her by the hand, they walked across the meadow.

When they reached the car the first light of day was breaking on the horizon, but it would still be several minutes before they sun would fully greet them. Right now, darkness continued to reign over the town of Raven's Peak.

Joe opened the passenger side door; the light inside automatically switched on, emitting its dull glow, as he helped Danielle into her seat. He walked round the front of the car and took a moment to look across the valley and down towards the woods. He clenched his fists and made a vow to return for the others, swearing he would not rest until his brother and friends were found.

Joe jumped into the driver's seat of the car. 'Don't forget your seatbelt,' he said while fastening his own. Danielle barked with a violent cough, projecting a black viscous fluid which spattered across the windscreen. She then began to have a fit, her entire body convulsing uncontrollably. She displayed the same symptoms as Tony had done the moment before he appeared to spontaneously combust and vanish. And then Danielle burst into flames. Joe's eyes widened. As quickly as the flames had erupted from Danielle's body, they died and in her place, hovering above the passenger seat, was a Shadowman.

In a panic, Joe reached for the car door, but his seatbelt locked, pushing him back into the leather. Before he could free himself the Shadowman placed its icy hand round his neck, its claws digging into his throat. Joe tried to pull the arm away, but as he did so its grip tightened. He then tried to kick and squirm free, but the seatbelt confined him to the driver's seat. He tried to reach for the seatbelt release, but the Shadowman was now sat upon him, trapping his arms underneath it. There was no escape.

The cabin light timed-out and the car plunged into darkness.

AUTHOR PROFILE

Duncan has spent most of his life in a small market town in West Yorkshire — the same town in which most of his stories are set under the guise of Raven's Peak. Duncan has been writing works of fiction since the age of seven. In those early days his stories often himself and his friends being transported to fantasy worlds. However, as a teenager, Duncan fell in love with horror movies and his writing took a whole new direction.

In the late '90s, Duncan turned amateur director and started creating his own horror movies with no budget and a video camera 'borrowed' from his parents. Fast-forward some thirteen years later, Duncan turned to film-making once more, and the idea behind *Within the Dark Places* was born — initially as a screenplay. Unfortunately, adult responsibilities caused the project to end before it had really begun. However, Duncan felt there was merit in the story and so developed his concept into a novella.

Duncan works in financial services and lives with his partner and their two young children. He is currently working on a sequel to *Within the Dark Places*. He also says he has already planned enough stories to keep him writing for the next twenty years, and he never stops coming up with new ideas.

Publisher Information

Rowanvale Books provides publishing services to independent authors, writers and poets all over the globe. We deliver a personal, honest and efficient service that allows authors to see their work published, while remaining in control of the process and retaining their creativity. By making publishing services available to authors in a cost-effective and ethical way, we at Rowanvale Books hope to ensure that the local, national and international community benefits from a steady stream of good quality literature.

For more information about us, our authors or our publications, please get in touch.

www.rowanvalebooks.com
info@rowanvalebooks.com